Mimi-Marina

and the Magical Doll Shop

Also by Navita Dello

The Secret of the Ballet Book

Mimi-Marina

and the Magical Doll Shop

Navita Dello

To my son,
my special global citizen

Chapter 1

Mimi-Marina carried herself, her bruised-by-sneaky-stuff-that-wrenched-her-heart-and-her-mind self, to the breakfast table and tried to stand upright.

'Who invented *rules*?' she asked.

Mum kept on buttering her toast.

Her elder sister, Ivy-Lea, rolled her owlish eyes at the air in front of her.

'Tell you what? Mrs Latimore has suddenly turned mean on me.' Mimi-Marina's eyes darted between the two. 'She made me give up recess on Monday to write lines and lines of "I, Mimi-Marina, will not forget my homework." She said the next time I'd have to part with a whole week of recesses for a larger dose of the same treatment, as if she knew there would be a next time.' Her throat tickled, knowing this wasn't the first time she'd failed to hand in her weekend work. 'Why does homework have to be done by 10 o'clock on Monday morning?' she asked. 'What's wrong with 11 o'clock on Tuesday?'

Nobody said a word.

Mimi-Marina's tone reached a few high notes. 'Why am I the only person in this family who is *ruled* by rules?'

'Not the case.' Mum patted her buttered toast with her knife. 'Shop owners do have to stick to the rules set by the authorities. And I have to get the orders done on time to keep the shop from running out of dolls of so many countries.'

Mimi-Marina swallowed. Mum did work hard. Even on Sundays when the doll shop was closed, she buried herself in the paperwork Dad would have done, had he lived.

She squinted at her sister.

'Pin your ears back for this one,' Ivy-Lea said. 'What could be worse than not being allowed to put my name down for the school play until I had handed in all my assignments for this term? Pack it in, kiddo.'

Mimi-Marina nearly dribbled. How could anybody who was an itsy four years older than herself keep calling her kiddo? 'I wish those were doughnuts,' she said, taking it out on the bowl of apples.

'An apple is better for your health,' Mum said.

Mimi-Marina's lips quivered. 'Fat lot of good it did Dad.'

Mum and Ivy-Lea exchanged glances as though *she* wasn't there. Yikes, why did that make her feel left out? If only Dad was around. To squash the sudden lump of pain in her throat, she wolfed down her fruit and nut wheat flakes. Then she shot off her chair as if rules might strap her to her seat.

'Your turn to clear up breakfast,' Ivy-Lea reminded her.

'Do I have to?'

'On the topic of clearing,' Mum said, 'Mimi, your room is a disgrace.'

Rules poured from Mimi-Marina's nostrils as she grabbed the cutlery off the plates. She hadn't even got over last weekend yet, what with Mum refusing to tweak her bedtime when Auntie Lyn came to dinner on Friday. Didn't it count that Auntie Lyn was her favourite aunt and the main contributor to her buy-something-tops fund?

Mimi-Marina went on loading the dishwasher noisily, her mind flicking to Sunday when she'd been whisked away from Chloe's sleepover party before any of the others were. Why did Mum have to arrive just as she was figuring whether to be Lady Mimi-Marina May, which was far cooler than being ordinary Miss, to fit into Chloe's *Lady of the Manor* theme for the morning?

Did rules always have to sneak up on her and ruin everything?

'If there's a page in the rule book for party-going as well,' she blurted, 'now that the school holidays are here, why don't we write in a rule that commands us to jet around the globe like what Hailey is doing, or –' Mimi-Marina bit her lip. She hadn't meant to bring up the holidays because she knew Mum couldn't afford to take them anywhere; she hadn't wanted Mum to feel bad.

'Not in a plane, but you could globe *trot* too,' Mum said. 'Help me out at the shop, and we can call you the assistant shopkeeper of the Global Village Doll Shop.'

Mimi-Marina couldn't believe her ears. Mum never let her hang around the shop during term time in spite of it being below their upstairs apartment. She narrowed her eyes. 'What are the shop rules?'

'Oh, the usual. Say *cheese* to the customers, hook the customers – see what I mean?'

Mimi-Marina didn't hear her brain booing the shop rules. And if that sort of rule was all, she would be in a near rule-free zone. A far cry from school and home. But she could sense Ivy-Lea pouncing again on the chance to call her a kiddo. 'I'm well past the doll stage,' she said.

'You won't be playing with the dolls,' Mum said. 'You'll be managing them.'

Mimi-Marina giggled, picturing herself bossing the dolls. Of late, Mum the shop owner had been far more entertaining than Mum the mum. She licked her lips. Urm. Managing. She also rather liked that word. It made her feel that *she* was the rule maker.

Mimi-Marina stood chest forward and all. 'Okay, everybody. Say hello to the new assistant shopkeeper of the Global Village Doll Shop.'

In her mind she smiled from ear to ear. Wasn't it last week Mum had said some dolls on the shelves were not posing the way they had the evening before? As if the dolls could gad about! Last night she'd been hilarious, claiming she'd spotted tiny marks on the shop floor, as if the dolls had frolicked.

How could Mum make such remarks looking deadly serious?

Chapter 2

On Monday morning, Mimi-Marina stepped out of her bruised-by-sneaky-stuff-that-wrenched-her-heart-and-her-mind self, and into her assistant-shopkeeper self.

She was going to do her job tip-top. She'd show Ivy-Lea the wannabe actress with no job that her *kid* sister could nail hers. The rest of Sunday she'd spent doing her homework, not boring school homework, but her job-related homework. The globe Dad had given her had come in handy to look up the countries she didn't know. She also did a bit of research on the Internet and memorised a few foreign words that meant hello.

She was better than ready to tackle the customers.

While Mum unlocked the cash register, Mimi-Marina darted to the front of the shop and twisted the board on the glass door so that the *opened* side faced the road. Surely, shop assistants didn't have to be told the basics. Then her gaze travelled along the lines of the shelves that covered the sea blue walls of the octagonal shop. She hadn't thought of it before, but Mum was right; it did feel like globe-trotting. Not just because the shelves were packed with dolls from different countries, either. It had to do also with the colour and the roundish shape of the shop.

She watched Mum rearrange the Tahitian dolls in their aqua grass skirts. Those dolls were so cool with a large yellow flower on each side of their heads. Mimi-Marina grinned. Mum chased detail; she was adjusting even the garlands of silky flowers around their necks.

Mimi-Marina skimmed the shelves for other dolls that might need redoing, and her eyes settled on the Australian aboriginal dolls in their traditional prints. The dolls in red headbands did need straightening. Yes, especially the ones wearing dresses made of fabric in lines of pink and red dots. She reached for them. Then she drew back, blinking. She'd never noticed those dolls glow before. She peered at some of the other dolls; they were glowing too. Unwittingly, her eyes sought the ceiling. Ah, silvery lanterns. Mum's new lighting – what an effect it had on the dolls.

She swirled to give Mum the thumbs-up, but the phone got to her first. Mimi-Marina's next step was to do a trot around the shop to familiarise herself with everything before the customers came in. With the shelves all labelled with country names, it had to be quick and easy. And so it was, until she got to the only panel of wall in the shop that hadn't been fitted with shelves. For a second, she stood with her feet stuck to the floor, and then galloped to the niche in that wall, her lips forming a *wow*.

'How long have you sat here?' she cried.

The big doll in the niche was wearing a dress made of crisp, white organdie petals, and on her head was a band of dainty white posies. Her feet, snug in white lace socks, were tucked into a pair of shiny white patent leather shoes, which also had posies on top. And her long hair that looked as if it had been bathed in golden syrup made Mimi-Marina want to hide her hair of short, coppery waves.

She bent forward and peeked into the doll's blue eyes that twinkled like sapphires. A momentary wisp of enchantment swept through Mimi-Marina's body. Quickly, she glanced at the lanterns again. Ooh, Mum sure knew how to create the right atmosphere for a doll shop.

'Mum,' she called, but just then the door opened, setting off the bell as a customer entered.

Mrs Williams turned out to be a regular who wanted a doll for her niece's birthday. While Mum was serving her, another customer traipsed in with a little girl clinging to her skirt.

Mimi-Marina was at their side in a jiffy, determined to sound like a real assistant. 'How may I help you?' she asked.

'Oh, hi. Bella is after –'

'The doll in pink with a parasol – nooo, the green one with a fan!' Bella skipped to the Japanese dolls in their richly worked silk kimonos. Then she was on to a Dutch doll in a blue dress with a white lacy apron. She couldn't take her eyes off the doll's wooden clogs which had windmills painted on top.

The lady beamed. 'You've got the whole world here.'

'That's why the shop is named the Global Village,' Mimi-Marina said.

Finally, they were on their way to the sales counter,

with Bella clutching the Japanese doll with the fan.

'You could say "Konichiwa" to your doll,' Mimi-Marina said to Bella. 'That's one way of saying hello in Japanese.' Then she gave herself ten red stars for doing her homework.

'You've got an efficient worker, here,' the lady said to Mum at the counter.

'I am the new assistant shopkeeper,' Mimi-Marina chipped in, making Mum laugh.

As soon as the door closed behind them, Mimi-Marina stole back to the doll in the niche. She didn't want Mum also to think *she* was a kiddo, so she lowered her voice to a whisper to speak to the doll. 'Are you a flower?'

The doll winked.

Mimi-Marina sprang back, gasping. *What was that?* She fluttered her eyelids and slipped up to the niche again, staring.

The doll returned her stare.

'Phew!' Mimi-Marina rubbed the pointy bumps that had erupted on her arms. How could she have let Mum's spooky remarks and the magical setting she had created get to *her*? She shook her head rapidly to shed whatever was going on inside. That got her thinking.

Was this how it felt the first day on a job? A warning bell rang in her ears. She mustn't tell Mum; it would look as if *she* couldn't cope with a few silly utterances and some light fittings. She was not going to be out of work in one day and let Ivy-Lea smirk.

She could hear the shop getting busy. Great. She'd join the buzz to keep her from visiting events that took place only in fairy tales. She wasn't going to be accused of feeling overwhelmed.

Once the shop went quiet again though, her stomach wobbled. She leaned on the counter. 'Things seem kind of different. Guess it's because I haven't nipped in here for about a month ... Mum, when did you get that big doll in the niche?'

'A few weeks ago,' Mum said, reviewing the price list.

'But why buy a flowery doll for a global village?'

'Didn't mean to.' Mum smiled sheepishly. 'Saw her in one of the catalogues, loved her – couldn't focus on the other dolls till I had ticked the box next to that doll.' She circled various items on the price list. 'Anyway, we may have to add another line of dolls to our collection to give customers more choice. If she sells, I'll get more.'

Soon there were customers again, more children too,

due to the school holidays. Mimi-Marina was glad. But when the shop emptied, she eyed the niche from a distance, and it put the wobbles back in her stomach. 'Get a grip,' she muttered. Then as if to prove that she had, she tiptoed right up to the doll.

Again the doll in the niche did nothing but stare.

Mimi-Marina stood frowning at the doll, lost in a jumble of disappointment and relief. Then she heard Mum call.

'I was wondering whether to shift this to one side.' Mum was tapping the roof of the dollhouse on the stand at the centre of the shop. 'It might make the shop roomier. With the kids coming in –'

'Then they won't be able to walk around it, Mum. How is it that you never sell this dollhouse?'

'Oh, well, it's meant to be a part of the décor.'

Mimi-Marina peeped through the windows at the wooden furniture and waved her finger at the wee dolls. 'Where are those dolls from?'

Mum appeared thoughtful. 'Well, they could be from any country, really. Everyone needs a home of some sort. The dollhouse depicts that in a way, I suppose.'

At closing time, Mimi-Marina gave herself an order: investigating the mystery of the winking doll had to stop. Starting now. How could she allow even her own mind to mock her for harbouring the notion that a doll could wink?

Without a backward glance, she followed Mum to the staircase to go up to their apartment. Then suddenly she swung round and dashed to the niche. She inhaled an extra-large portion of air and gaped at the doll.

The doll winked.

Chapter 3

That night, Mimi-Marina lay in bed hugging a pillow to her chest as if that would curb the tidal wave her evening's thoughts had created. But her mind kept flowing. Was it possible to imagine a doll had winked not once, but twice? Then again, maybe she had, in a bigger way than she cared to admit, allowed her mind to play with Mum's comments which implied the dolls pranced around the shop at night. Also there was her first-day-on-the-job thing.

Then what was that unusual vibe in the shop?

Mimi-Marina scrambled out of bed. If something was going on, shouldn't she find out? Luckily, she didn't have to pass Mum's room to get to the stairs that led to the shop. The problem was Ivy-Lea. She placed her ear against the wall adjoining her sister's room. Nope, tonight Ivy-Lea wasn't being Scarlett from *Gone with the Wind*, or Maria from *The Sound of Music*, or anyone from anything else.

Hastily she changed into her jeans and yellowy tee-shirt that lay crumpled on her chair, and tiptoed along the passage and then crept down the stairs. Not a sound, not a movement. Yet as soon as she opened the door, that fleeting moment of magical strangeness that had engulfed her in the morning came to her. Stronger.

Tiny shivers whizzed through her body.

She fumbled for the switch in the darkness and put on the lights. All appeared the same. She stood with her feet twisting inside her shoes though, letting only her eyes flit here and there.

Nothing weird.

Mimi-Marina beat her path around the dollhouse. Now she could see the flowery doll in the niche. Her pulse throbbed, but she edged forward until she was facing the doll.

Still, nothing.

Go on detective, her mind poked her. Then she

lunged at the doll and peered into her eyes that seemed bluer than during the day.

The doll blinked. Once, twice.

Mimi-Marina jerked her head and nearly fell back with her arms held out.

'I was hoping you'd come,' the doll said in a sing-sing voice. 'My name is Petal.'

Mimi-Marina's heart thumped. 'I'm,' she said, and gulped. Then she gripped her jeans and started again. 'Mimi-Marina May, n-nine years old, the new assistant shopkeeper.'

'I gathered that, by the way you were bustling around helping the customers.'

'I've never met a doll that talks for real!' Mimi-Marina said.

'Well, now you have! Tippertyda-tippertydo.' Petal slipped off the niche.

To stop her from falling, Mimi-Marina stuck her hands out but they dropped to her sides, and she watched wide-eyed.

Petal was climbing down invisible steps to the ground. Then she craned her neck and looked up at Mimi-Marina.

Mimi-Marina sank to her knees at once so she could

be level with Petal.

'That's better,' Petal said. 'We can talk.'

Mimi-Marina slid closer to Petal as if to ensure she didn't miss even a pause. 'Are you a magic doll?'

'You could say that. But correctly speaking, a *semi-person*,' Petal said in a voice that was showered with pride. 'In with the humans, in with the dolls – that would be me. Get the gist?'

'Er, urm, I think so.' Mimi-Marina drew a deep breath, trying to make sense of what Petal was saying. 'I didn't know there were semi-people. Is there a semi-person in every shop?'

'Goodness, no. That wouldn't be possible.'

'Then what made you come to *this* shop?'

'It's not up to me,' Petal said. 'It's our queen's decision.'

'You have a queen?' Mimi-Marina now pinched her thigh to confirm she wasn't asleep. 'A real one like the Queen of England?'

'Queen Alexandra of the Dolls lives in a palace and travels in a golden carriage drawn by white horses. How much more real can it get?'

'Still, why did your queen decide to send you here to Mum's shop?'

'Here's the thing.' Petal wound a strand of her syrupy hair around her weeny finger. 'The queen can turn only a small number of dolls into semi-people. So the one way she can allocate them to shops fairly is to put the doll shop owners through a test.'

Mimi-Marina gave a start of surprise. 'Did my mum do a test?'

'Urm, she doesn't know she did a test, but she sort of did,' Petal said. 'Queen Alexandra observes doll shop owners around the world. She picked your mum as one of the owners who is dedicated to bettering the overall well-being of dolls.'

'Oh, yes, Mum is always improving the place and making it cosy.'

'There you go! The queen also has an eye on owners who pay attention to things like display and stocks to meet customer demand.'

'That's Mum! She starts the morning off by shifting the dolls around for best effect. She is also like a hawk when it comes to keeping an eye on stocks and placing orders.'

'So you see?' Petal flung her little arms wide. 'In fact, the queen values anything that promotes sales as the survival of the doll community depends on humans wanting them. The more dolls out there in the hands of humans, the less chance they will be forgotten. The greater the chance they will be appreciated and sought after. That provides continuity for dolls. That's what Queen Alexandra holds dearest to her heart.'

Mimi-Marina's brain muddled through what she was hearing. 'Mum mentioned she got you recently,' she said at last.

'That's because your mum is now a *selected* one. The queen is all for hard-working and courageous people. That's why I was delivered to her.'

'*The Queen of Dolls made it happen!* Ah, that explains why Mum couldn't resist choosing you for the shop even though you didn't fit into the global theme.'

'Petals, flowers. Flowers and countries – no special connection?'

Mimi-Marina tucked a note in her head to Google the subject.

'Anyhow,' Petal said. 'The point is that a semi-person is sent by the queen to people like your mum to help them for a while.'

'In what way?'

Petal pointed at the dolls on the shelves. 'By bringing them to life.'

Mimi-Marina gawked at the dolls. 'They can talk too? Then why aren't they speaking?'

'Here's the thing,' Petal said. 'Unlike me, they have to be invoked with the power of speech and body movement to come to life.'

'Invoked? How?'

'I have to recite the code of life,' Petal said. 'Dolls that get to live are joyful souls – they emit happy energy which produces a glow.'

'I saw that glow!' Mimi-Marina grinned as if a bulb had ignited inside her own head. 'I thought it was the new lights.'

'Those glowing dolls look gorgeous, don't they? Great for boosting sales is that glow and for sprinkling the shop with magical delight.' Petal tapped her chest. 'That's how a semi-person like me assists a *selected* shop owner to promote the sale of dolls.'

'Do they come alive only at night?'

'Any day, any time. No restrictions.'

'Sweet,' Mimi-Marina said. No sneaky rules – these dolls' lives had to be uncomplicated and fun.

'However,' Petal said. 'We are not allowed to talk to adults. When adults are around, we can't speak to kids, either.'

'Er – '

'Oh, and the other rule is that only a semi-person is permitted to chant the code of life. It will be really dangerous for the dolls if anyone else recites the words in their presence. Now enough with the serious stuff!' Petal chortled. 'Tippertyda-tippertydo. It's time to introduce the dolls to you.'

Chapter 4

Petal ran her gaze around the shop as if to make certain that all the dolls were paying attention.

Posing like statues, how could they? And how could any kind of magic put life into those stiff-looking figures? In spite of her doubts, Mimi-Marina's eyes weighed in on the dolls when she heard Petal's voice.

Petal was swaying while in a rhythmic tone chanting the code of life:

'With the permission of Queen Alexandra of the Dolls, may you graciously adopt the code of life: Selato Dale life Manifica Brill life Cresato Atoon life Notari Zelene. Selato Dale life Manifica Brill life Cresato

Atoon life Notari Zelene. Greetings from the Queen!'

Mimi-Marina slapped her cheeks with her palms.

The miniature dolls at the top were now tumbling and turning, the shelves their playground. The littlies on the middle shelves were descending along invisible slides as though they were at a park. The big dolls on the lower shelves were, as Petal had done, climbing down steps that were not there.

Mimi-Marina stretched her eyes as far as they would go.

When all the dolls had reached the ground, Petal raised her hand above her head and waved it about. 'Listen, guys, I want you to meet Mimi-Marina May, the new assistant shopkeeper of this Global Village Doll Shop.'

The dolls circled Mimi-Marina and threw their arms up in glee.

Swept by the moment, Mimi-Marina stretched out hers to them, and two littlies climbed on to her knees.

'I have a suggestion,' Petal said to the dolls. 'You can introduce yourselves and give Mimi-Marina a nugget of information about your countries – one special thing. We'll hear a few of you each night. That way, there will be plenty of time for play before we wind off for the night.'

'Yahoo!' the dolls chorused.

The first to embrace Petal's program was a doll with a fringe and braided dark hair down to her shoulders.

Egypt, Mimi-Marina whispered to herself, easily recognising that look as this morning she had taken note of those dolls on the shelves because Mrs Latimore was discussing the wonders of Egypt.

The doll's long chunky earrings swung like pendulums when she moved. And the dazzling stones on her headdress and on the broad collar of her turquoise blue gown made Mimi-Marina blink.

'I am Cleopatra,' she said. 'Named after the last pharaoh of ancient Egypt.'

'The pharaohs,' Mimi-Marina cried. 'I've seen lots of pictures of the pyramids of Giza where some of the pharaohs were buried. And Mrs Latimore, our teacher, told us the largest pyramid was the oldest of the seven ancient wonders of the world.'

'The Pyramid of Khufu!' Cleopatra's smile reached her eyes. 'I can see you are interested in ancient Egypt. Here's another thing. Egyptians used a writing system called hieroglyphics. Instead of letters, they drew pictures to make words.'

'Writing in lines of pictures, how awesome! Even homework would be fun if we were allowed to do it with pictures instead of ABCs. I'll ask Mrs Latimore if we could – when she gets to the topic of hieroglyphics! That was a very special nugget of information. Thank you for sharing.'

The other dolls clapped.

'Who's next?' Petal asked.

The doll that stepped forward grinning was dressed in a red cotton skirt with a green apron edged in yellow. Over her white blouse she wore a broad black waistband.

She gestured at the others behind her. 'We are from Italy.'

'*Ciao,*' Mimi-Marina said, glad that this time she had only to come up with an easy-to-say hello.

The Italian dolls made cheery sounds.

'I've seen your boot-shaped country on my globe,' Mimi-Marina said. 'And Hailey, my classmate, went to Rome last holidays and visited the Colosseum. Ooh, gladiators fighting, blood spilling. Those must have been exciting times!'

'Ah, but I am named after the most beautiful spot in Italy, so I'll tell you about it,' the Italian spokesperson said. 'The place is called Venice and it is made up of mini islands that are parted by canals and linked by bridges. It's a city on water.'

'Wow, a whole city?' Mimi-Marina imagined houses and trees drifting on water.

'It's like a floating city,' Venice, the doll, said. 'So apart from walking along the streets, people travel in water buses, water taxis –'

'Lucky ducks! You should see how our car gets stuck at red traffic lights whenever I'm going anywhere *cool*, like to the movies, or a friend's. It sucks,' Mimi-Marina said. 'Thanks for your special nugget of information.'

The next to answer Petal's call was a peasant doll with long expressive eyes and a sizeable red spot on each cheek. She wore a shapeless dress hand-painted in a colourful floral pattern.

'I am Matriona from Russia,' she said.

'You clever people! Didn't the first man to travel into space come from there?'

Matriona smiled. 'That's our Yuri Gagarin.'

The red spots on the cheeks of the other Russian dolls around Matriona turned darker as if they were blushing with pleasure.

'*Matriona* is also the word from which we

33

Matryoshka dolls got our name. I will show you what is special about Matryoshka dolls.'

Before Mimi-Marina could even indulge in a breath, Matriona twisted her waist until her upper body got detached from her lower body and hung down. Then from inside her, another identical but smaller doll popped out.

Mimi-Marina felt her eyes bulge.

Then the second doll's upper body came off too and another doll emerged, and it went on and on until there were eight identical dolls – each one littler than the other.

Mimi-Marina now blinked rapidly as if to stop her eyes from rolling out of their sockets and on to her lap.

Matriona straightened her top half and let it spin until it fitted back to her lower body. 'As you can see, we are nesting dolls.'

'Do you nesting dolls always come in eights?'

'Usually. See, I am the mother, that's what Matryoshka means. These are my seven children. We are also called Babushka, for grandmother.'

'Sweet!' Mimi-Marina said. 'Thank you for your special story.'

Petal's hand went up again. 'Hey, guys, let's continue

with the introductions tomorrow. Off you go to play.'

The big dolls scuttled here and there – some in pairs, others in groups – and the littlies played games like hide and seek.

The tiny marks on the floor! Ah, this is how they got there; Mum hadn't been joking. Mum, Ivy-Lea. With all the excitement, she'd forgotten about them. What if either of them came down? Mimi-Marina glanced at the door, and then hurried to the staircase and listened out for a moment ... Quiet. From now on, she told herself, keep tuned into any sounds or movements upstairs.

Then she sat at the centre of the shop by the dollhouse watching the dolls play and chatting to Petal, who perched beside her. She couldn't help reflecting on herself with her friends in their school playground at recess.

After a while, Petal skirted her way into their midst. 'Okie-dokie, guys, we have been up longer than other nights. Don't we have to look fresh and bright when the shop opens in the morning?'

'Yahoo!' the dolls said. Then they scurried to the shelves and climbed unseen steps to get to their places.

'I have to recite the code of dolls to turn them back to ordinary dolls,' Petal whispered to Mimi-Marina.

Could such active dolls become statues? Just as Mimi-Marina was about to hoot at her own changed opinion, she was jolted by a thought. Suppose the dolls remained playful? What with Mum already suspicious...

To the same catchy tune, Petal was now chanting the code of dolls:

'With the permission of Queen Alexandra of the Dolls, may you graciously adopt the code of dolls: Selato Dale doll Manifica Brill doll Cresato Atoon doll Hetari Jemene. Selato Dale doll Manifica Brill doll Cresato Atoon doll Hetari Jemene. Farewell from the Queen!'

The shop fell silent.

The shop turned still.

Mimi-Marina could hear herself breathe.

Then she clapped as if a show had ended. She hugged Petal. 'Thanks a whole billion for letting me meet the dolls. It was the *yummiest* night of my life!'

Petal winked. 'Tippertyda-tippertydo. See you for another night of cavorting tomorrow.' With that, she climbed to the niche.

Mimi-Marina waved at her.

Petal didn't wave back.

It appeared she'd shed the semi-person in her and

become a doll.

Mimi-Marina reached for the light switch at the staircase, but fidgeted. What if Mum detected a difference again in the way the dolls posed? She peeped over her shoulder.

As far as she could tell, the dolls looked the same as earlier.

Mimi-Marina went upstairs pretending the steps were invisible. The wondrous part of the school holidays was going to be the nights ...

Chapter 5

Mimi-Marina lay in bed grinning in the dark. Ivy-Lea with a boyfriend at the mall? Well spotted, Chloe! And thanks for texting me. So *flawless* Ivy-Lea was also keeping a secret from Mum. A secret boyfriend. Who would have thought?

Mimi-Marina drew her feet right up to her body and her duvet formed a sort of pyramid on her bed making her feel like a mummified pharaoh. 'You know more about the dolls than I do,' Mum had said during dinner. Mimi-Marina chuckled. She'd spent a whole week listening to the dolls tell their tales, hadn't she?

She turned sideways to check her bedside clock and

the pyramid collapsed, which got her wondering how the pyramids of Egypt had lasted for thousands of years ... 'Sleep, Ivy-Lea,' she muttered. 'It's past Mum's bedtime too.' But tonight she could hear her sister moving around in her room. She was probably practising to walk the red carpet in high heels at the Oscars.

Mimi-Marina got back to her pyramid-position. She'd ask Cleopatra how the pyramids were built to last so long. Now she could feel the rhythm of the code of life. She could hear the words too. Petal must think she was not coming. And *she* didn't want to be left out of the fun downstairs.

Unable to hold back another minute, she opened her door as softly as she could and crept from her room. Ivy-Lea's door opened at once.

'What are you doing prowling around at night? Sneaking food into your room, are you? You know Mum doesn't like – '

'And how will Mum like your having a *boyfriend*?' Mimi-Marina cut in.

'Boyfriend?' Ivy-Lea went pink. 'Oh ... you mean one of our cast members.'

'Then you must have been *practising* at the mall to

hold hands with Aladdin!'

Ivy-Lea's face now looked as if it was turning into a beetroot. 'You can't tell Mum!'

'Then *you* can't tell Mum I was trying to have a midnight feast.'

'Promise.'

'And you can't call me kiddo from now on. Never!'

Ivy-Lea's *owly* eyes glared. 'Promise,' she managed.

'You're on!' Mimi-Marina said. 'But aren't you going to tell Mum about him?'

'Of course, I will.' Ivy-Lea chewed her lip. 'Er, when I'm sure ...'

Although she'd struck a bargain, Mimi-Marina slipped back into bed scolding herself for trying to steal past Ivy-Lea's room when she was awake. Ivy-Lea had a nose that could smell a rat on another continent. *She* was asking for trouble; she had to be more careful.

Mimi-Marina kept staring at their adjoining wall. In her head, Petal's chanting was still going on.

Ivy-Lea's room had gone quiet ...

'Oh, there you are!' Petal darted to her when Mimi-Marina stepped into the doll shop. 'Tippertyda-tippertydo. We got started because we thought you were not coming.'

'Sorry I'm late.' Mimi-Marina scooped up Petal and then settled on the floor by the dollhouse. 'I couldn't get past my sister's door till she finished rehearsing for the Oscars.'

At that, a doll with a shiny purple stone and a dot on her forehead rushed to Mimi-Marina, almost falling over some littlies. She wrapped herself in the soft plum silk that was draped over her right shoulder after being wound around her waist. 'Is your sister a Hollywood movie star?' she asked.

Mimi-Marina tittered. 'She's on about making it in Hollywood.'

'And I'm Meena, a Bollywood movie star doll from India.'

'Namaste!' Mimi-Marina smiled not only at Meena who was holding her palms together in front of her chest, but also at her own memory for retaining how to say hello in Indian.

It was too late, however, for the usual introductions.

While Petal chatted to a group of dolls, Mimi-Marina watched the others. What a pity she hadn't got down in time for Petal's chanting which could wake up anything. Inwardly she swore at Ivy-Lea, ignoring that swearing was against Mum's and Mrs Latimore's rules. *She* had just missed the most magical part of the night. The moment the dolls came to life.

Thanks a lot Ivy-Lea for making me miss the beginning. Then the on-going rhythm in her head reached her lips and silently she began mumbling the code of life …

All at once, every doll from every country was sprawling on the floor.

No chatter.

No laughter.

No play.

'Oh, noooo!' Mimi-Marina lurched forward on her knees to get to the dolls.

Petal grabbed the dolls she'd been speaking to and shook them. They fell back lifeless like rag dolls. 'Can't happen! Can't happen! The code of life recited by a semi-person cannot be broken … unless … unless … a human repeats it … human, *girl* –' Petal's eyebrows shot up in a questioning slant.

'*Girl, did you stop the world spinning?*'

'I – I –' Mimi-Marina's heart fell to bits. 'I only –' She swallowed a sob. 'I only whispered under my breath. Th-they couldn't have heard a word of the code.'

'You broke the rule!' Petal screeched. 'I told you that only a semi-person is allowed to chant the code of life. I told you it will be dangerous for the dolls if others around them recited it. It makes no difference *how* you recited it.'

Oh, yes, oh, yes, Petal had even called that rule serious stuff. Oh, what had she done? Mimi-Marina cringed, wishing she was the teeniest doll in a set of Matryoshka dolls; she'd be hidden eight times then, before anyone got her. 'I'm sorry, I'm sorry. I didn't realise the rules were *seriously* serious.'

'Of course rules are serious. Don't humans have to follow rules?'

'We do.' Mimi-Marina could barely hear her own voice.

Petal folded her arms in front of her. 'Everybody has to live by some rules. Otherwise, they would do as they please, as you have done.' She pointed her elbow at the shop floor. 'And this is how it ends up.'

Mimi-Marina winced at what looked like a mass of dead bodies from countries of all the continents. She *had* stopped the world …

'Wake up, oh, please, wake up,' she cried. Then she twisted this way and that, and tugged and prodded the

43

dolls around her. Again, there was no point. Then she buried her face in her palms and sat sobbing her heart out ... After a while a ray of hope dried her tears a little. 'Hang on. I can't be certain, but maybe what I recited was the code of dolls. The rhythm is the same as the code of life – and the words are similar, aren't they? That could be why the dolls stopped living.'

'Can't happen!' Petal's tone was crisp. 'A human cannot *invoke* that code.' Then her small body began trembling and her voice cracked. 'The d-dolls won't be able to talk any more.'

'*Ever?*' Mimi-Marina spluttered.

'Ever.'

Mimi-Marina burst into tears again. 'C-can't you do anything?'

'I can't,' Petal wailed. 'The only one who can is Queen Alexandra of the Dolls.'

Mimi-Marina dared to breathe again. 'Please, please go to her. Tell her it's *my* fault and that I'm sorreeee.'

'Won't work,' Petal said. 'The one who can ask her for forgiveness is the one who broke the rule.' She stared at Mimi-Marina without blinking.

'*Me?*'

'You are the person who could try to correct this

mess, though not so easily because here's the thing. Once a human has dabbled, urm, interfered with the code of life, the queen's power to intervene is limited.'

'Limited?' Mimi-Marina yelped. 'How limited?'

'The queen can't just accept your apology to save the dolls,' Petal said. 'To return the dolls to life, her value-system has to trigger a forgiveness signal – which comes from a genuine feeling from her heart to forgive. To receive that signal, she has to be convinced without a spec of doubt that you deserve to be forgiven ... You have to win her heart.'

Mimi-Marina's head bulged with rules. The dolls had more rules than humans. Big, freaky ones.

'You know what all this means,' Petal pressed on, 'because I've already explained how the happy glow of dolls that can live helps sales and also radiates mystical magic around the shop.'

'And now all that will be lost! Oh, Petal. Mum has to make the shop work. With Dad gone, she has to. The shop is the only thing we've got.'

Petal stretched her arms as far as they would go around Mimi-Marina's waist and made soothing sounds. Then the sadness etched in her face deepened. 'There's another thing ... Although there's no rule that says a child can't hear the code of life, it was still an error of judgement on my part to let you, given the danger, as I told you, of anyone other than myself reciting the code to the dolls. So considering that I was sent here to bring the dolls to life, the queen's value system is bound to persuade her to withdraw my semi-person status, and turn me into an ordinary doll that can't talk.'

'Nooo!' Mimi-Marina said. 'Surely she'd forgive at least you. You've got to try.'

'The queen's limited power to set things straight makes it tricky for me as well. The queen can't forgive me just so that I can retain my semi-person status to keep the shop going by bringing to life the new dolls that are delivered to the shop. Again, her forgiveness has to come from her heart – she has to feel the signal.' Petal heaved a sigh. 'She is stricter with the dolls than she is with humans about matters relating to the workings of the Doll Realm. That will make it doubly hard for her to forgive me, without you first persuading her to forgive you, which would put her into a compassionate mode that'll soften her heart.'

Mimi-Marina threw her arms around Petal. 'Don't be scared Petal! I'll go to the queen, and I'll make her forgive me. Somehow. Where is she?'

'At her palace in the Realm of Dolls.'

Chapter 6

Mimi-Marina's brain hammered against her skull. 'How do I get to the Realm of Dolls?'

'Humans have to be escorted by semi-people,' Petal said. 'I'll have to travel with you. And we must go at once because the queen won't be able to revive the dolls if they are left in this state for too long.'

Mimi-Marina imagined Petal calling for a carriage driven by horses, somewhat like the queen's. She strained her ears for the sound of wheels and hooves going clipperty-clop.

She heard nothing except Petal's voice.

'No one must see the route to the Realm of Dolls for

the protection of Queen Alexandra's palace,' Petal was saying. 'So the realm rules require that we keep our eyes closed till we get there. Now brace yourself, and take my hand.'

Mimi-Marina clasped her hand in Petal's and shut her eyes. Petal began mumbling some magic. Mimi-Marina could barely hear it, but she zipped her lips so that this time she couldn't as much as hiss.

The muttering kept going ...

Then with a jerk Mimi-Marina was lifted off the ground. She waited for her head to bump into the ceiling. But no. She was rising, rising ...

She tightened her grasp on Petal.

Had they reached the clouds? Or gone beyond?

Her stomach squirmed. She hadn't been even in a plane before. What if they crashed into one? Or were on the path of a rocket? Her clothes stuck to her with the warm sweat beads that were trickling down her body. Shouldn't it be freezing up here? Seized by the unfamiliar, she opened one eye a fraction. She shut it, spooked by the dark and continued into the oddness.

Rising, rising ... making her stomach angrier, nastier. Wicked.

Petal?

Where was Petal's hand?

She stretched her arm. Still no Petal. A gong clanged in her ears. She stuck her other arm out as well.

Petal was nowhere.

Mimi-Marina was going down.

Down ...

Down ...

Chapter 7

Mimi-Marina was lying on something. Soft, like a mattress. A mattress? Her eyes flew open.

She was on a bed.

The squeaking bed wasn't hers.

Nor was the bedroom with scribbles on the wall.

The sun was pouring in through the window. She recoiled. Where was the night sky? Where was Petal? Where was *she*?

She couldn't feel her breath; even that had abandoned her. She leapt off the bed, her skin turning creepy-crawly at the sight of more things that didn't belong to her. Clothes lying on the floor, shoes sticking out of the cupboard, socks hanging from the drawers ...

Her own room was better than this; this room was rule-free. Why didn't that at least give her any comfort?

Mimi-Marina picked her way past the lumps on the floor to get to the door and burst out of the room. The narrow, empty corridor she was standing on didn't as much as hint at her whereabouts. She raced along the passage and ended at a spiral staircase. Peering down the stairwell made her giddy. She clutched the wooden rail and bounded downstairs. Not a soul. Then she hammered on a door and yanked it open. No one.

Last of all she wound up in the kitchen.

'Thought you decided to stay on in the Land of Nod.'

'Where am I? Where's Mum?'

The woman at the table surveyed the ceiling and then pointed at herself. She had pea-green eyes that couldn't pass off as brown. She had a pug nose that couldn't pass off as pointed. She had crinkly hair that couldn't pass off as straight.

She was nothing like Mum.

'Where's *my* mum?'

'C'mon, sleepyhead, aren't you overdoing it? Tuck in.'

Why was this woman pretending to be Mum? Before Mimi-Marina could untangle her tongue, there was a tap on her head.

A round-faced boy around thirteen, Ivy-Lea's age, was shoving her out of the way to get to the table. 'You wouldn't pass on grub would you, kiddo?'

'How dare you call me kiddo,' Mimi-Marina said. 'Only my sister, Ivy-Lea, is allowed to.'

The boy and the woman cracked up.

'Did you adopt a sister?' the woman asked. 'Ivan, cut me a slice of that mud cake, will you?' She glanced at Mimi-Marina. 'Go on, drop the bad mood and have some of those treacle tarts before your brother gobbles them.'

'He is not my brother! I don't have a brother! Where –'

'And I'm not your mama, right?'

'You're not! *My* mum doesn't let me eat junk food for breakfast. She makes me have nutritious food like fruit, cereal –'

Ivan cracked up again.

'Nutritious?' Mama said. 'Oh, Millie, you've been listening to far too many health nuts on telly.'

Mimi-Marina choked on an empty throat. 'I'm not Millie, I'm Mimi-Marina May. Tell me where I am!'

'Mimi what? C'mon, time for school. You could leave

with Ivan if you get your act together.'

'I want to go home, not school!'

'Oh-ho, so that's what it is! Having one of those off-school days, are we?' Mama patted her chin with two fingers. 'Why didn't you say so? Maybe you will feel like going to school tomorrow.'

Mimi-Marina felt her eyebrows twitch. Mum would have freaked out at the prospect of *her* missing even half a second of school. 'Aren't there any rules about going to school from Monday to Friday?'

'Rules?' Mama sounded as if she'd never heard the word.

'I don't have time for Millie's clowning, I'm off.' Ivan gave the woman a peck on her cheek. 'Bye, Mama.' He swung out of the kitchen.

Mimi-Marina stared after him. What were these people up to?

'Now, honey-pot, we can have a chinwag at home,' Mama said.

Mimi-Marina crammed her lungs with air. 'I'm not Millie, I'm not your honey-pot, I don't have a brother, and I don't want to be *here*!'

With that she banged the door and bolted out of the house.

Chapter 8

Mimi-Marina stood outside the house appraising the other buildings in the neighbourhood. No, she didn't dare knock on a door and get sucked into another weird home. She looked left. Dead-end. Forest. She checked right. Ivan was swinging along in the distance. She'd head up the road too and ask the first person she bumped into how to get home. Her real home.

Mimi-Marina trudged along the pavement, stamping on the weepy feelings that were swamping her. How did she get here – had Petal got the magic words wrong? If that was why she was, er, blown into that house, then why wasn't Petal here too? Why was only *she* here? And why was that peculiar pair pretending they knew her?

Soon she was jabbing her face to wipe away tears that insisted on coming. Petal must be wondering what had happened to her. How was she going to rescue Petal and the other dolls when she was stuck here? Oh, how?

She raised her hands to her ears and grimaced at the traffic; why were cars revving and horning to get past? They were disturbing her thoughts. She panted. Where was everybody? Didn't people take to the pavements here? Now she could see Ivan turning in. That had to be the school. From what she could fathom, slinking in there could be the only way to speak to anyone ...

Mimi-Marina entered the school grounds. From nowhere, a girl came charging up to her looking as if she'd stepped out of a box of glitter.

'Howdy!' she said. 'You're staring at me. My *newy*, isn't it? What do you think of Gala, the party girl?'

Gala's navy blue checked sequin shift dress reminded Mimi-Marina that she was still in her jeans and old, meant-to-be-salmon-pink tee-shirt which had faded into a palette of pinks. Not that it mattered if kids were allowed to come to school in their party gear.

Gala twirled around. 'It's comfy too. You should get

one, Millie.'

Millie? Mimi-Marina let out a nervous grunt. It had to be Mama; she would have informed the school to expect her daughter. That could be even the reason she'd suggested school ... But then, why was Gala behaving as if she, Mimi-Marina, was her friend, Millie?

'The bell's gone, let's get to class,' Gala said.

Mimi-Marina's feet got ready to dash off. Then the empty pavements flashed in her mind. At least here there were people; there had to be someone outside of her class she could speak to. What if she left without trying and then ended back with Mama?

Mimi-Marina went with Gala.

As soon as she got to class, it was Millie this, and Millie that. Mimi-Marina's eyes prickled. She'd been reduced to a computer file that had been renamed. She drummed her fingers on her desk. Was Petal at the palace? Petal had said they had to hurry. Was it too late to save the dolls?

And herself – from being Millie?

Then an enormous P on the board distracted her. The teacher was writing words beginning with P and next to them sketching the corresponding pictures. Pig, pot, pen … Mimi-Marina nudged Gala on her right. 'Are we learning a type of hieroglyphics?'

'Hiero …? Oh, that lot is just for the kids who are still on Ps. Mrs Merriday's drawings keep going way out of shape, don't they? Glad we're done with the three-letter words.'

'Three-letter words!' Mimi-Marina almost fell off her chair. She couldn't be in the wrong class because the children were around her size. She twisted to double check the students behind her. No *smallies*. But why were some swaying with earphones plugged in? Why were some sitting on desks and chatting? Why were others playing games?

Why were there no class rules?

'Jasper, have you got your Ps right?' Mrs Merriday was looking at the freckly boy sitting next to Mimi-Marina on the left.

Jasper turned red.

Mimi-Marina leaned sideways and stared at Jasper's book. He'd written the Ps the wrong way round. It threw her off her seat. 'Watch me,' she said, and wrote a huge neat P very slowly in Jasper's book. 'Try it.'

Jasper wrote a whole line of Ps below Mimi-Marina's. 'Thanks,' he mumbled with an eagerness that lit his eyes. Then he filled the rest of the page with lines of Ps.

As the day went on, Mimi-Marina's hopes of speaking to someone at school got dimmer. How was it that even the teachers and kids of other classes not only knew Mille but also thought she was Millie? They were never going to believe her story.

She wriggled around in her chair and let her mind run amok ... The police ... the police, they'd get her home safe. Why hadn't she gone to them in the first place? Her heart did a little hop. Now she could see that Jasper was far off from a solution to *his* problem. Basic additions. He was counting with his fingers as she had done when she was barely out of nappies. Her hand shot up. 'Mrs Merriday, which exercises do we have to do for homework?'

The whole class guffawed, except Jasper.

'Since when did we take school back home?' Mrs Merriday asked.

That's why the kids barely know how to write or juggle with numbers, Mimi-Marina wanted to yell. How was the world going to produce the next Lewis Carroll or the next Isaac Newton whom Dad had always gone on about? She clamped her mouth. She had to focus on getting out of this place. If she didn't, it would be the end for the dolls, for Petal, and for the doll shop.

When school was over, Mimi-Marina pounced on Gala. 'Where is the nearest police station?' she asked in a carefully planned casual tone.

Gala made a frowny face.

'The police – the people who make sure we stick to rules?'

'Haven't seen any police-people around here,' Gala said.

Mimi-Marina's heart sank. Leaving Gala behind with her frown, she tore out of the school. No police? And no one who accepted that she was someone other than Millie. Mimi-Marina trembled right down to her toes.

Would she ever get out of this place?

She strode along the pavement, the cars on the road now bugging her more than in the morning. Engines revving, horns tooting, brakes screeching ... and then – *bang.*

Crash!

Chapter 9

Mimi-Marina screamed. At the junction, two cars and a van had collided. Crowds were gathering; people were shouting. 'The boy,' she heard some say. Then the deafening sounds of a siren …

She crept through the mob and pushed her way forward. Then lying on the road, she saw the boy.

She knew him, she knew him!

The boy was Jasper – the only kid in the class who wanted to learn.

As he was lifted on to a stretcher, he barely moved. Mimi-Marina's insides rattled from crying. Why didn't these vehicles stop at the red lights, the way they did back home? Every minute in this place was making her wither, making her die.

She belted all the way back to the house that was supposed to be her home. She'd shriek day and night if that's what it took to get that fake mama to accept that *she* wasn't her Millie, that *she* had to be sent back to her real home.

Mimi-Marina scampered into the kitchen, but there was no sign of Mama. What was awaiting her was a sink full of dirty dishes and a table stacked with party food that hadn't been cleared since breakfast – a rule-free kitchen. But as with the rule-free bedroom, it brought her no comfort. Without thinking, she threw herself at the sink and splashed the dishes in water until they squeaked.

Then she stormed upstairs to her room, fell face down on the bed and wept into the pillow. How did she get here? Where was she? And why? What she did know was that Mum would be sick with worry. Mum would have found the dolls on the shop floor and her daughter missing.

'I'm here, Mum,' she sobbed, 'living in a house with no rules, attending a school with no rules, and they are all in a town with no rules.' Wasn't that supposed to breed a life that was uncomplicated and fun?

An image, an image was flashing ... flashing ... flashing in her mind. Active bodies from loads of countries were falling dead on the floor. That's when Petal had asked her whether she had stopped the world spinning ... She sure had.

And it was all because she hadn't followed a simple rule: why had she chanted the code of life when Petal had told her she mustn't?

Mimi-Marina shoved her nose farther into the pillow as the images kept changing. Petal? Oh, her body stiff, her eyes hollow. And Mum. Mum. Her face creased with money worries. Was that how they were going to end up because of *her*?

As the pillow got damper and colder, Mimi-Marina wrenched it away and faced the wall. If only it was that easy to escape from the fact that she'd treated rules carelessly and it had become a habit. So much so, that she couldn't help herself even when warned that the consequences would be grave.

She turned on her back. *'I want to return to my life with rules, and save the world!'*

Her ears crumpled to what sounded louder than thunder, and her body shuddered to what felt windier than a gale. The window burst open and she staggered to it.

How was it already dark outside? The sky was blacker than usual, possibly as there were no stars. She gaped into the darkness until in the distance she saw something white. It was as if the stars had left to give way to whatever it was.

Mimi-Marina kept staring. It was getting closer. 'A ball!' Enormous. Sort of a full moon in white. She resorted to quick, short, sharp breaths.

The white ball-like thing was coming ... coming ... coming towards her.

But her feet had gone heavy; she couldn't move aside. 'Stooooop!'

The ball, which now looked mammoth, kept coming.

She clung to the windowsill and was about to squeeze her eyes shut when she saw an illuminated message forming on the ball.

It had to be for her!

The ball hovered above the window.

'Phew!'

Mimi-Marina leaned over and read the gold-lettered words on the ball.

'Catch the loop to rise, and close your eyes and keep

them shut till you feel the ground.'

Just then from beneath the ball popped a ring-shaped loop fixed to the end of a chain in white. Dividing the black sky, the chain dropped until it was dangling by the window.

Mimi-Marina flung her arms and grasped the loop. She closed her eyes. Tight.

She was lifted out of the room and into the night sky.

Chapter 10

Mimi-Marina moved her right foot in slow, deliberate circles to ensure she was on solid ground. Then she allowed her eyes to open ...

She was standing in the middle of the Global Village Doll Shop.

Glaring at her, with her hands on her waist, was Petal.

'Where were you?' she squealed. 'You went missing in mid-air, so I came back here.'

'I ended up in the wrong place!' Mimi-Marina said, collapsing on to the floor in a heap.

'Impossible, I was guiding you.' Petal's blue eyes

pierced Mimi-Marina as if they were looking inside her to get to the root of what had happened. 'All *you* had to do was hold my hand and keep your eyes closed.'

'I did, I did. Was only when I got really, really scared that I opened my eye a –'

'*Goodness!*' Petal's hand flew to her forehead. 'I told you that no one must know the route to the Doll Realm.'

'Don't worry, I didn't see anything. I remember you told me to keep my eyes shut till I got to the palace. But I panicked, I'm sorry. I just kept going. Up, up. Then after a while I got dumped somewhere weird.'

'The queen's security system must have done that,' Petal said. 'It would have detected that someone was watching the path to the realm. Then it would have diverted that person, er, you, back to where you came from –'

'*Is that how it happened?*' Mimi-Marina gasped. 'At last I've hit on the answer to my mysterious flight path and landing. Except that I didn't get sent back here! Where I touched down was another place full of strange human beings.'

'The security system must have made a mistake,' Petal said in a quieter voice. 'How the system works is this – its sensors pick up the main qualities, moods of guests who are checking out the route to the realm, and accordingly transport them back to their worlds. However, if the system can't quite locate such a place, urm, maybe due to the extreme tendencies of some guests, then they are sent to surroundings created more or less according to their traits.'

Created! She'd been in a town, a rule-free zone, which had been invented for her. No wonder all the people there behaved as if they knew her. Mimi-Marina's cheeks burnt. How could she whinge at the security system for deriving the idea that a place with no rules was *her* world?

'Then how did I get back?' she asked in a mousy voice.

'Here's the thing,' Petal said. 'The queen's security system doesn't mean to leave anyone stranded. You must have sent *some* kind of signal indicating you'd been dropped off in the wrong spot. Did you?'

'I, er, might have,' Mimi-Marina whispered. 'I just might have ...'

'There you go. The system would have picked up your distress call and returned you here, based on what it newly sensed about you.'

'Luckily!' Mimi-Marina then turned her gaze to the shop floor. 'How come the dolls are still where they fell? Didn't Mum come into the shop this morning? Was she upset? Was she worried about me?'

'The time you spent in your, urm, parallel human world could be different to the time that ticks here – it's still the night that we left for the Realm of Dolls.'

'Oh, sweet! Then with luck it won't be too late to save the dolls, so let's hurry.'

Petal's face turned as white as her dress. 'It may be fatal to take you to the palace now that you've broken *two* rules.'

'I'll explain to the queen! I'll –'

'It's not that easy once you are faced with the double-rule principle.'

'Double-rule?'

'Remember, I told you that the queen's value system has to trigger a forgiveness signal, a sort of heartfelt desire to forgive you in order to be able to return life to the dolls?'

Mimi-Marina nodded.

'And that even the queen's power to intervene is limited once a human has messed with the code of life?'

Mimi-Marina nodded again.

'Well, for starters, as you've broken two rules, there's a greater chance that her value system won't be able to grant you forgiveness –'

'We must go, try! We must.'

'Here's the thing.' Petal's shoulders drooped. 'If the queen is unable to pardon you, it won't be only the dolls, the shop and me that will suffer – now *you* will too.'

'Like how?'

Petal coughed, went silent and then coughed again.

Mimi-Marina suddenly felt she was standing at the edge of a cliff. Why was Petal stalling? What could be so bad?

'If the queen's heart is not softened by your plea,' Petal finally said, 'the double-rule principle requires that she turns you into a *doll*.'

Mimi-Marina's heart thudded. 'She can't change people into dolls! She can't, she can't!'

'The queen has been known to transform serious doll-rule breakers into dolls.'

Mimi-Marina's knees quaked, and her jaws locked, trapping her words. Then her mind nudged her about something Dad used to say whenever she had a whopping maths problem at school: 'Go step by step.'

'What happens if I *don't* go to the palace?' she asked, taking the first step.

'You'll be safe because you are not in the Realm of Dolls.'

'But the dolls won't be able to talk again, and Mum's shop will lose its magical vibe,' Mimi-Marina said.

'That's right.'

'And you?' Mimi-Marina asked, moving on to the next step.

'I am under oath,' Petal said. 'Even if you don't go to the palace, I still have to visit the queen and tell her about my own error of judgment in letting you hear the code of life.'

'Then you'll be in trouble as well.'

'I told you that unless the queen's compassion has been roused by forgiving you, she won't be inclined to excuse me. Her heart won't allow it.' Petal's face twisted with pain. 'So for me it will be the same issue – losing my semi-person status and becoming an ordinary doll that can't talk.'

Mimi-Marina gulped. 'From what I can see, if I don't go to the palace, you lot will suffer and only I will be safe. If I go to the palace but fail to be forgiven, like you all, I'll be in trouble too because the queen will t-turn me into a doll.'

'That's what it amounts to.'

Mimi-Marina's head reeled. How could she sit tight and let the others suffer when she was the one who had broken the rules? As if to help her with her final step, blood gushed into her brain and washed out the fluff.

'But, if I go to the queen and succeed in convincing her to forgive me, we will *all* be safe. What are we waiting for? Take me to the queen!'

Petal studied Mimi-Marina's face with probing eyes. 'You mean it, don't you?'

Mimi-Marina's nodding made her head move in huge ups and downs.

'Tippertyda-tippertydo.' Petal sounded her usual self. 'Then take my hand and close your eyes.'

Chapter 11

Mimi-Marina dug her heels into the ground and opened her eyes. She was standing in front of a milky white marble palace studded with hundreds of arched windows. Crowning the palace was a dome that was gigantic and gold.

She ogled the building but couldn't stop her mind yo-yo-ing between fairy-tale palaces and prisons. Would she ever get out of there as a girl? Wincing, she turned to Petal. Then from her mouth poured a string of shocked utterances for Petal was almost as tall as she was. Mimi-Marina's hands flew to the top of her head. 'What's happened to me?'

'You've shrunk,' Petal said. 'You had to. How else would you enter the palace?'

'Will I get back my usual height?' Mimi-Marina yelped.

'That depends,' Petal said, 'on your persuading the queen to pardon you instead of changing you into a doll.' She tucked her arm around Mimi-Marina's waist.

It felt just as if Chloe or Hailey was comforting her.

'This is your last chance to back out,' Petal said. 'I can still take you back to the shop if you wish. Once we go into the palace if things don't go well, it will be the point of no return.'

Mimi-Marina's heart went bump. Why had she allowed the situation to become a horror movie? Before she could talk herself out of going inside, she lifted her chin and said, 'I'm no cowardy custard!'

'Then follow me.'

The guard standing at the entrance to the palace had a moustache that curved upwards. He was dressed in a long, chalk-striped jacket that had brassy buttons.

'Enter,' he boomed when he saw them and he held the door wide open.

Petal marched through and, hiding behind her, Mimi-Marina shuffled in.

She could hear her heart now beating in staccatos, in spite of the bustle of the dolls around them. 'How is it that a few of those butlers and maids are that much taller than the others?' she asked.

'Not sure,' Petal said. 'They could be the ones that the queen converted to dolls.'

Mimi-Marina shuddered, and looked away at once.

Then Petal led the way along a maze of white carpeted corridors that seemed as though no one had ever set foot on them. Finally, they reached a hall where a few dolls sat silently by an intricately carved door. In front of it was another guard like the one that stood outside the palace.

'The door to the queen's parlour,' Petal whispered, elbowing Mimi-Marina towards it.

Then they too were seated to be called. Waiting hustled Mimi-Marina with scary ifs and buts. To fence them off, she tried to count the crystals on the chandelier above their heads. But her mind insisted, instead, on conjuring pictures of Mimi-Marina the doll stepping out of the queen's room.

After all, she was already as short as a doll.

'Enter,' boomed the guard when it was their turn to meet the queen.

Then Mimi-Marina and Petal set foot in the parlour which had paintings on every wall, and a floor that was laid with furniture upholstered in silvery white. And on each table were china figurines that reminded Mimi-Marina of the dolls looking like statues on the shop shelves. Her eyes ducked every which way to dodge the figurines, but they seemed to watch her from all angles of the room. Freaking out, she glanced up, and the dome that was glistening because of its gold elaborate design made her eyes sting.

Then at the far end on a throne decked with gems was Queen Alexandra of the Dolls, looming tall.

Mimi-Marina felt shorter than before.

The queen was wearing a heavy robe made of the whitest velvet and trimmed in gold. She sparkled with the diamonds around her neck and on her crown.

Mimi-Marina peeped at Petal from the edge of her eye. Then just like Petal, she curtseyed to the queen.

'Rise,' the queen said in a lofty voice. Then with a haughty sniff, she stretched out an arm at Petal. 'Say, what you have come to say.'

'Oh, Your Majesty,' Petal began. 'We are having some trouble at the Global Village Doll Shop. Mimi-Marina, here, chanted the code of life and the dolls stopped talking and playing. I can't revive them.'

'That tells me you let her learn the code although it must never be uttered by human lips.' Queen Alexandra swiped her head with a circular movement. 'You know your role is to bring the dolls to life so that they glow and become more popular among humans. You know very well that the one way the doll community can survive and thrive is if humans buy them. You also know that I can vest semi-person status in only a small number of dolls to bring together both realms – humans and dolls.' The queen threw her head back. 'Your behaviour has been unworthy of that trust. I will divest you of your semi-person status.'

'Your Majesty, please don't! Please hear me out,' Petal said. 'Though semi-people usually can't introduce the dolls to the owners or managers of the doll shops as they are adults, here was an assistant shopkeeper who is a child. And I thought if I let Mimi-Marina meet the dolls, it would be good for the shop.' Petal took a tiny two steps towards the queen as if it would help to get through to her. 'On Mimi-Marina's very first day at work, I noticed how enthusiastic she was about the doll shop and the customers. She was able even to say hello in languages of several countries relating to the dolls. It got me thinking that if she mingled with the dolls, she could do really well in promoting sales to enable our continuity.'

The queen's face looked rocky. There appeared nothing forgiving about it.

A surge of panic heated Mimi-Marina's body. Her only hope was that the queen was less strict with humans as Petal had said.

Then the queen eyed Mimi-Marina whom she'd ignored all this while.

Her cold gaze made Mimi-Marina freeze. It didn't feel as if it was going to be easier for her to soften the queen's heart.

'Girl, I see you've been working at the doll shop,' the queen said. Her voice was as icy as her eyes. 'Yet you didn't adhere to the rules of dolls.'

'I'm sorry, Your Majesty,' Mimi-Marina said. 'The dolls have become my friends, *dear* friends. I never meant to harm them. The rhythm of the code was so magical, thrilling, I got caught up in it. Now I know that rules are rules.' Mimi-Marina leaned forward. 'Even if you are angry at me, please think of my mum, the owner. She's been working seven days a week to keep the shop going since Dad died. Our family needs the shop to do well. Mum needs a semi-person, and she needs me.'

The queen held her hand to her heart and closed her eyes.

Mimi-Marina gave Petal a slit-eyed look.

'She's searching for what's in her heart,' Petal whispered.

Mimi-Marina kept her eyes skinned to the queen. A grimace, a frown, a smile – they could all say something.

Those faces didn't show up in the queen.

When the queen opened her eyes though, Mimi-Marina saw a flicker. Was it understanding? Empathy? Oh –

A sudden bleep made Mimi-Marina jump.

The queen peered at her palm.

'Oh, goodness,' Petal whispered to Mimi-Marina. 'That's the queen's security system communicating with her.'

Soon the queen emerged from her palm, and her face was harder than rock. She pointed a long bony finger at Mimi-Marina. 'You are the only person to arrive from another realm, today. It has to be you who was diverted from our route for observing it!'

'I'm sorry, so sorry, Your Majesty! I was terrified in the sky and – '

'Stop!' Again with her menacing finger, the queen gestured at Mimi-Marina. Then she puffed up, becoming increasingly towery on the throne.

Mimi-Marina now felt knee-high.

'Girl, you will be subject to the double-rule principle because you've broken two rules,' the queen said. 'I will turn you into a realm doll, and then you will serve me at this palace!'

Oh, no, she was never to return home! Mimi-Marina's body went stiff. Then that stiffness began spreading right down to her fingers and toes as if she was changing into a doll. Now she couldn't even tremble her terror away.

Petal rushed right up to the queen. 'Please, Your Majesty. Consider Mimi-Marina's courage. She decided to come here and ask you for your forgiveness in spite of knowing that if she didn't come to the palace she'd be safe at home. She cared about the dolls, she cared about me, she cared about her mum. And she cared about the prosperity of the doll shop which we know is vital for our continuity. For all that, she was willing to risk the possibility that she might be converted to a doll. Isn't that courage?'

Mimi-Marina didn't breathe, didn't blink. She knew what Petal was doing because Petal had told her that the queen valued courage.

Again the queen held her hand to her heart and closed her eyes.

Mimi-Marina immediately plunged forward and stretched her neck for a closer view of the queen to pick even a twitch that might serve as a clue ...

The queen's face looked masked.

Then she opened her eyes and shook her head slowly at Mimi-Marina. 'This is getting complex. Given the dire consequences of your action, I'll need a little help to search my feelings. I'll have to talk to her.'

Her? Mimi-Marina shot Petal a silent query.

To whom was the queen going to speak?

Chapter 12

'Before I talk to her, I am going to make both of you invisible, in two ways,' Queen Alexandra of the Dolls persisted. 'She won't see you, and you won't see her or me.'

Mimi-Marina pursed her lips to hold back a sob. She was itsy-bitsy as it was. Soon she'd be gone. What if the queen's heart told her to leave them invisible, forever?

The queen's eyes were fixed on Petal. She swept her hand in a zig-zag manner which created wispy bubbles in front of Petal.

Mimi-Marina blinked. *Petal was gone!*

Then Mimi-Marina saw bubbles in front of her ...

She immediately launched an attack on herself: pinching, poking, jabbing. She was there – still pieced together in body and limb. A gush of relief flowed through her in spite of the not-being-seen part making her feel eerie. An eerier silence ticked ... Then she heard footsteps.

It had to be *her*.

'How is your work progressing?' the queen asked whoever it was. 'Tell me from your heart exactly how it is.'

'My sales are going well, and things have really picked up.'

Mimi-Marina stood on her head inside her invisible self. *That voice!*

It belonged to Mum.

Had she known about the Realm of Dolls all along? But how so if dolls didn't speak to adults? Mimi-Marina ditched her thoughts and juggled between an image of doll-sized Mum and the conversation she was having with the queen.

'How did you turn your shop around?' the queen was asking.

'Well, I've got lovely dolls to begin with. I guess this sounds crazy, yet they, urm, appear to glow.' Mum chuckled. 'And with the school holidays the children are coming in, and my little daughter is helping me cope. She has a great rapport with the customers – she even interests them in the dolls by telling them about the places the dolls come from. She must be doing some research as she seems to know an awful lot. Oh, she's such an asset to the shop.' Mum's voice was bubbly. 'Perhaps I am getting tied into the magic of the shop. Yes, my shop has this new feel – a sort of vibe. I'm not sure how it got there, but I'm not complaining ...'

Why wasn't the queen telling Mum that it was semi-people who created the vibe? Why wasn't she telling Mum about Petal? Again Mimi-Marina blotted out the questions popping into her head to stay on top of what was being said.

'Congratulations on your success with the shop,' the queen was now saying. 'Keep it up.'

Mimi-Marina heard a rustle and then footsteps, which faded away. Then she saw Petal standing right next to her and peering at the queen. The queen was again with her hand to her heart and her eyes closed.

And it went on ...

Oh, why was she taking longer than before? Hadn't Mum's words touched the queen's heart? Mimi-Marina stood rigid as if she was rehearsing to be a doll.

Gradually, the queen opened her eyes and gazed at Mimi-Marina.

Her eyes shone, and her face flushed with the softness of silk. When she spoke her voice was dripping with kindness.

'Girl, I understand you have been a great asset to the doll shop and a mountain of strength to your mother,' she said. 'My heart is telling me to forgive you for breaking the rules.'

'Oh, thank you, thank you Your Majesty –'

'I have a request,' the queen said.

Mimi-Marina held her breath.

'Once you grow up, you won't remember the Realm of Dolls or anything relating to it, including the code of life. But while you are a child, you must never let other humans learn the code and never tell them about the magic of semi-people. That knowledge belongs to the Realm of Dolls.'

Mimi-Marina swallowed, recognising the responsibility she now bore. 'I promise, I won't tell anybody else,' she said solemnly. 'Now I understand that if the code of life is used incorrectly, it will affect the dolls and the demand for them among humans.

Surely, that would hinder Mum's shop too. Please rest assured.'

The warmth from forgiving Mimi-Marina still showed in the queen's face and eyes when she turned to Petal. 'You should have consulted me first before allowing a human into the processes of the Realm of Dolls. Yet given that as a semi-person your main goal, rightly, was to secure the future of the doll community, I can see why you made that decision. It has caused trouble, but it has also had a positive outcome. Bear in mind that you are never to let other humans learn the code of life. On that basis, I'll forgive you.'

'Thank you, Your Majesty,' Petal said, curtseying deeply.

'Come here now,' the queen said to Petal.

When Petal tiptoed to the throne, the queen held out her hand. 'Chant the words on my palm to the dolls. Keep at it.'

Yahoo, Mimi-Marina mouthed, the way the dolls cheered.

'But,' the queen added pensively. 'To get that glow, you may have to wait till the new stock of dolls arrives because if the lifeless dolls don't bounce back when you recite this verse that means it is too late for them.'

Chapter 13

'I'm back to my real size!' Mimi-Marina said when she opened her eyes at the shop and looked down at Petal. 'Now to rescue Cleopatra, Meena and the gang!'

'I'll start the reciting right away,' Petal said.

Mimi-Marina sat on her knees with her eyes hooked on the dolls that lay dead-stiff all over the shop floor.

Petal chanted the magic verse.

The dolls didn't budge.

Petal repeated the magic.

Not a stir.

'I know I got the words right, but the dolls aren't coming to life,' Petal cried. 'I think it's too late!'

'Try a little louder.'

Petal raised her voice …

Yet the dolls appeared to have gone to sleep for good.

Petal covered her face with her hands. She sobbed so hard her shoulders shook.

Mimi-Marina gave her a cuddle and then stroked her head while her own eyes welled with tears. What exactly did the queen say? She tuned into the queen's voice – first icy and then kind once she had found it in her heart to forgive. Mimi-Marina focused on that kind voice telling Petal to chant the words on the queen's palm. Was that all? Something was missing. What? What? Then she grabbed Petal by the waist. 'Keep at it Petal, keep at it!' she said. 'The queen told you to "Keep at it".'

Petal stopped sobbing and sniffed. 'Did she?'

'She did, she did! Go on!'

Petal stood with her shoulders back. This time she kept on chanting the words … chanting … chanting …

Mimi-Marina kept her eyes glued to the dolls.

After what seemed a decade, a big Mexican doll's hand fluttered.

Mimi-Marina landed on her feet, hopped over some

other dolls and then nearly lost her footing on a sombrero to get to the Mexican doll that was wearing a red and blue crocheted dress. She knelt right beside the doll. Now the doll's foot was wriggling. Soon, she lay stiff again … Then her leg slid sideways a little. She raised an arm but it dropped, and she uttered a grunt. She tried again and reached the ribbons that were knotted into her hair and tugged at a red one. Then she rubbed her eyes, and with a jerk sat up.

Mimi-Marina cried a happy sob and gave the doll a giant hug.

Petal went on, and on, and on …

One by one, the other dolls too started coming to life.

Petal didn't stop chanting until they were all up and about. Then she dashed to the dolls crying, 'Are you guys all right?'

'Think we fell asleep,' Venice said, sounding vague.

'Sweet!' Mimi-Marina grabbed Venice and bounced to her feet. Then she spun round and round holding the doll in her outstretched arms.

'Tippertyda-tippertydo,' Petal said.

Then as it was still dark outside, Mimi-Marina sat by the dollhouse with Petal and watched the dolls.

The shop floor was a playground again.

Soon Mimi-Marina's head was buzzing with some of the questions she'd shelved. 'I was stunned when Mum arrived at the palace,' she said. 'Didn't you say dolls didn't speak to adults? And without a semi-person, how did Mum get to the Realm of Dolls?'

'Only the queen can speak to a *selected* one,' Petal said. 'The queen doesn't speak to other adults, and can't instruct other humans to come to the Doll Realm unless they are brought to her, as you were. But I bet it's rare for the queen to get a *selected* one to come to the realm. That's why, I was also confused when she kept referring to *her* ... The queen must have decided that the situation warranted her use of her special powers.'

Mimi-Marina fluffed Petal's gold locks and beamed. 'I'm glad you can stay on as the semi-person of this shop.'

'Here's the thing,' Petal said, in a whispery voice. 'Although the queen can make certain that a semi-person gets to the shop she has chosen, she has no control over how long the semi-person can remain at that shop.' Petal's lower lip curled. 'Dolls that are invoked as semi-people to protect the continuity of dolls through helping selected shop owners increase sales will only be semi-people while they are performing that function. If they are sold and taken away from the shop, then they will lose their semi-person status and become ordinary dolls.'

'That's not fair!' Mimi-Marina cried.

'Oh, well, that's because they can no longer perform the task for which they received that semi-person status. The queen doesn't have the power to give life to dolls except for a specific reason. But for every semi-person she loses through sales, she can invoke a new one with that status to maintain the numbers.'

'Then what about the dolls at the realm, who were talking and walking about?'

'They are the realm dolls,' Petal said. 'They have been given life for the purpose of serving the queen and the Realm of Dolls. If they leave the realm, they too will become ordinary dolls.'

Mimi-Marina lifted Petal to her lap and snuggled her. 'Oh, Petal.'

Petal looked up at Mimi-Marina with the spark gone in her eyes. 'The idea is to give the shop a boost, which is expected to make it viable for the future. The queen naturally hopes that the semi-person will stay on at the shop for as long as possible to bring the dolls to life and keep them glowing. Yet nothing is forever ...'

I'm having a ghastly dream, Mimi-Marina whimpered in her mind, but just then, she felt Petal quiver in her lap.

'Once I'm sold,' Petal said. 'I'll become an ordinary doll that can't talk.'

Chapter 14

Next morning Mimi-Marina's head felt too heavy to lift off her pillow. Petal, an ordinary doll? No, no. Petal had to talk; Petal had to walk; Petal had to play. Petal had to bring the other dolls to life. Yet how was she going to stop Petal from getting sold?

Petal was on the price list. Besides, Mum had said she might add other types of dolls to the shop and was going to test how well Petal sold ... Then Mimi-Marina lurched to a seated positon. Now that Mum had been to the Realm of Dolls, would she be open to the suggestion of not selling Petal?

She banged her head back on the pillow. The

problem was the queen's request. Not being allowed to tell anyone about semi-people meant she couldn't explain to Mum how important it was to keep Petal for the sake of the shop.

Mimi-Marina peeked at her clock and slid out of bed, her brain fishing in her head for ideas. She had to come up with a plan. But what? She yanked a pile of tee-shirts from her cupboard. Then her eyes captured what had been hiding behind them.

Her treasure box.

Mimi-Marina wrenched the box open and plucked out a long, cream envelope, and gave it a pat. 'Thanks a bunch, Auntie Lyn, for your generous contributions. They have totted up to a meaty buy-something-tops fund!'

Ivy-Lea changed roles all the time, didn't she? *She* would do it too for a baby minute this morning. She put up her best customer voice. 'Hi, there,' she said. 'I, Mimi-Marina, would like to buy the doll in the niche.'

Then nobody else could buy Petal.

Using Dad's method, in her mind she ticked off step one of her new save-Petal project.

Then she sat at the computer. Step two. She had a hunch that the research she'd put off up to now could be useful to make certain that Petal held on to her semi-person status for as long as possible.

Nothing was forever – Petal had said so. Mimi-Marina's heart missed a beat. But Petal was right. Just as Queen Alexandra had said that *she* wouldn't remember a thing about the Doll Realm once she grew up.

After searching the Internet, Mimi-Marina bounded into the kitchen. 'Mum,' she called.

The person who answered her was Ivy-Lea.

'Mum is not opening the shop till afternoon –'

'What?' Mimi-Marina asked, as if she was hard of hearing.

'Mum has gone to Auntie Lyn's. She's had a fall and can barely hobble.'

'Then I want to see her as well! And I also need to speak to Mum.'

'Me too.' Ivy-Lea was chewing her lip again.

It had to be the boyfriend thing. Mimi-Marina watched Ivy-Lea's eyebrows gather. Having a boyfriend seemed like an awful lot of trouble. *She* was not going to have one! 'So you've decided on Aladdin, then?'

'He is *not* Aladdin! Anyway, Mum's arranged for Chloe's mum to come and pick you to go to their place today. She should be here any minute. Got play practices, myself.' Ivy-Lea sped off mumbling her Jasmine lines from *Aladdin*.

That night, Mimi-Marina crept down to the shop. It sucked that she'd returned from Chloe's to find that for the second time she'd missed telling Mum that she wanted to buy Petal because Mum had returned to Auntie Lyn's after closing the shop. Still, she couldn't wait to tell Petal her plan. That had to put the sparkle back in Petal's eyes.

Mimi-Marina swung round the dollhouse almost knocking it off its stand. Then she halted.

The niche was empty.

Her stomach went funny. Then a few not-again noises shot out of her mouth. Did Mum really have to keep moving the dolls around? Trust her to think of some new form of display. Mimi-Marina sighed and strolled around the shop with a roaming eye. 'Petal?'

Not a sound.

'Stop being funny, we're not playing hide and seek. Can you hear me?'

No reply.

Mimi-Marina zoomed in on the shelves. Not on the

top shelves. Not on the middle shelves. She squatted on the floor and checked the lower shelves where the other big dolls were. 'Petal, are you there?'

No again.

It was so not like Petal to hide away in fear, so that couldn't be it. 'Where's Petal?' she asked, glaring at the dolls as if it was somehow their fault that Petal had gone missing. Then she clutched her coppery waves and stamped her foot. Without Petal to invoke the code of life, she wasn't going to get a word out of these dolls.

Then Mimi-Marina's brain churned out a reasonable answer.

Petal could have been sold.

Boo! Boo! Mimi-Marina inwardly spat and kicked. How could that be? The shop hadn't been opened for longer than a teeny-tiny afternoon. Again, she scanned the shelves, scanned the floor, scanned the area by the cash register.

Petal was not in the shop.

Mimi-Marina flopped on the floor and wept.

She'd been too late to save Petal from turning into an ordinary doll that couldn't talk.

Chapter 15

In the morning Mimi-Marina's eyes were sore from crying. If she stepped foot in the shop, that empty niche was sure to make her throw up. But how could she tell Mum she wanted to quit? Now with no semi-person, the shop would need her even more. And wasn't Mum relying on her?

She dragged herself to the kitchen to check on Auntie Lyn. Mum was humming a tune. Oh, did she have to? Mimi-Marina's stomach knotted as if to warn her that listening to merry music too would make her sick. Besides, it wasn't like Mum.

'All ready for the slog?' Mum joked.

Mimi-Marina wasn't in the mood for humour, either. What was wrong with Mum?

Then as though she knew what Mimi-Marina was thinking, Mum said, 'I'm not sure what's got into me – since the night before last.'

'*The night before last?*' Mimi-Marina stood at attention and ready to salute. Was Mum going to let on she'd been to the Realm of Dolls? 'Did you go anywhere then, er, I mean, anywhere extraordinary?'

'Of course, not.' Mum's animated laugh ripped round the kitchen, increasing Mimi-Marina's desperation for a bucket to be sick in.

'Got sort of inspired about the shop,' Mum said.

'Isn't that quite normal for you?'

'No. I mean the hands-on thing. I want to put my thoughts for the shop – which I have been sitting on since Dad died – into action.' She scrunched her forehead. 'I don't know what it was about the night before last ...'

Mimi-Marina gave her a long searching look. It appeared that Mum felt something had happened, but she couldn't remember ... Then Mimi-Marina whistled under her breath. So that's what it was: Mum didn't recall the Realm of Dolls because she was an adult, just in the same way that the realm would fade from *her* memory when she grew up. Ah, and there was the answer to why the queen didn't tell Mum about semi-people and Petal. Even though Mum was a *selected* one, what would have been the point if it was all going to fizzle away from her mind when she left that realm?

'Guess I'm going a bit barmy,' Mum said, barging into her thoughts. 'It's been hectic with all the work I've been putting into the shop. You also have. In fact, with the kids coming in and all that, you've been indispensable. You have become a very special part of the Global Village Doll Shop.'

Mimi-Marina went warm and melty inside which momentarily eased her pain. By discovering the semi-person of the shop, she probably had become even more special than Mum realised. 'Maybe Dad somehow knew I'd be important to the shop,' she said. 'Could that be why he gave me that globe?'

'Possibly,' Mum said with a teary eye. 'That reminds me – hold on.' She skittered out of the kitchen and got back in a tick with a parcel. 'It was the night before last also that got me to properly address what a great job you've been doing. So here's a present from me too.' She handed the package to Mimi-Marina. 'Thought I'd give it to you now to enjoy because you have only a week left of your school holidays.'

'Oh, Mum, you didn't have to get me anything.' Mimi-Marina tried to pump some joy into her voice. Nothing could make up for what had happened. Yet getting that Mum would expect her to open the parcel, she placed it on the table and reluctantly unwrapped it.

Then she gazed into a pair of eyes so like blue sapphires. They belonged to a doll dressed in white organdie petals.

The doll was Petal.

'Mum! Mum!' Mimi-Marina flung her arms around Mum. 'The *best* gift you could have given me, Mum, the best. She is sweeeeet!'

Mum doubled over laughing. 'That brought a smile to your face this morning, didn't it? I know you're past playing with dolls. Yet I've seen the way you gravitate to her whenever there aren't customers in the shop. Have to admit I also lost my heart to her!'

'Mum, I have an idea,' Mimi-Marina said, curling her fingers into fists knowing that Petal's fate depended on Mum's answer to her question.

'Why don't we let Pet, er, this doll be a part of the décor in the shop?'

'I thought you could place her in *your* room. Perhaps on the window seat. I could order in another doll or two of her type to try out for my new line.'

'But, Mum,' Mimi-Marina said. Wasn't she glad she'd done her research for step two of her save-Petal project? 'Remember you said the dollhouse is décor and the dolls in it could be from *any* country as people everywhere need homes? This doll also represents all countries because she is a flower, really. Just look at her! Stacks of countries have flowers as symbols.'

'Oh, you mean floral emblems?'

'That's it!' Mimi-Marina reflected on the list of national flowers she'd complied. 'The cantuta for Peru, the peony or the plum blossom, I think, for China, the rose for England and America – '

'The golden wattle for Australia,' Mum added with a broad smile.

'Exactly what I mean. Pet, er, this doll *does* fit into our global theme.'

'You've learnt a lot since you became the assistant shopkeeper! I'm proud of you.' Mum planted a hug on Mimi-Marina's head. 'You know what? You seem to have grown up a little if that's possible in a week – become more responsible ... I guess we could make a few changes to your bedtime, TV time and so on.'

'*Really?*' Mimi-Marina high fived with Mum. 'And my idea?'

'Love it! I'll grab it! Are you sure?'

'Of course. I won't have much time for other things once term starts, anyway.'

'Well then that's settled,' Mum said. 'Your doll will sit in the shop, and if customers enquire about her, I'll order some in. Aren't I excited? We may be expanding our vision for the shop!'

'Mum, can I talk to you?' Ivy-Lea was standing in the doorway. Then before following Mum out of the kitchen, Ivy-Lea exchanged glances with Mimi-Marina.

Suddenly, Mimi-Marina felt *included*. 'Sweet!' she said, raising Petal up in the air.

Petal winked at Mimi-Marina.

Mimi-Marina returned the wink.

Thank you for buying this book

If you enjoyed reading *Mimi-Marina and the Magical Doll Shop*, please consider leaving a review wherever you bought the book.

Thank you in advance. Your support is truly appreciated.

Best wishes,
Navita Dello

Also by Navita Dello

The Secret of the Ballet Book

Sierra cannot believe her luck when a dancer steps out of her ballet book and offers to train her for the audition that might spare her from having to quit ballet. However, unless the dancer forever re-enters the page within the deadline set by the witch who trapped her, she is fated to disappear. Would Sierra succeed not only at the audition but also in getting the dancer out of the book for good? Or would Sierra end up inside the ballet book too? Worse still, disappear?

37437689R00065

Printed in Great Britain
by Amazon